The Perfect Gift

MARY NEWELL DePALMA

ARTHUR A. LEVINE BOOKS
An Imprint of Scholastic Inc.

For Arthur A. Levine, editor extraordinaire

Text and illustrations copyright © 2010 by Mary Newell DePalma

Library of Congress Cataloging-in-Publication Data
DePalma, Mary Newell.
The perfect gift / Mary Newell DePalma. — 1st ed.   p. cm.
Summary: Lori the lorikeet wants to give her grandmother a present, but after dropping her beautiful red berry into the river, she and her friends must try to retrieve the berry or find another gift.
ISBN-13: 978-0-545-15402-4
[1. Parrots—Fiction. 2. Animals—Fiction. 3. Gifts—Fiction. 4. Grandmothers—Fiction.
5. Books and reading—Fiction.] I. Title.
PZ7.D4385Per 2010 ✶ [E] —DC22 ✶ 2009006769

10 9 8 7 6 5 4 3 2 1   10 11 12 13 14

The art for this book was created using acrylics.
Book design by Elizabeth B. Parisi

First edition, January 2010 ✶ Printed in Singapore 46

Little Lorikeet
  found something
that the larger lorikeets
  had missed!

"I will take this to my grandma," she thought.

But it was not easy.
She stopped to rest.

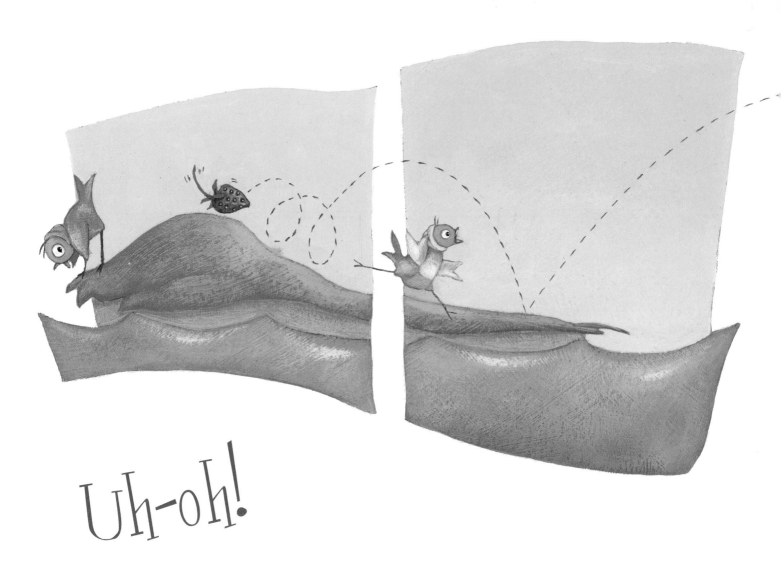

Uh-oh!

Her beautiful strawberry started
to roll.
It hopped.
And finally, *plop!*
It sank right to the bottom
of the river.

Lori began to cry.

A chipmunk skittered to a stop.
"What's gotcha so sad?" she asked.

"Hip, hop, *plop!*" sobbed Lori.
"My beautiful red berry sank
right to the bottom of the river."

"Don't you worry now,"
the chipmunk chittered.
"We'll get it out of there!"

The chipmunk was brave.
She filled her little
balloon cheeks with air,
She strained and stretched,
but she just couldn't reach
the beautiful red berry.
Gulping and gasping,
She came up empty-handed.

"That beautiful red berry
was for my grandma," sighed Lori,
"and now I have nothing to give her."
Lori and the chipmunk slumped
on the riverbank and
thought for a while.

"Why so sad, my friends?"
asked a goose, gliding by.

"Hip, hop, *plop!*
Her beautiful red berry
sank right to the bottom of the river,"
said the chipmunk, "and we can't reach it."

"Maybe I can help you," said the goose.

She ducked.
She extended her lovely long neck,
her webbed feet waved,
and her tail stuck
straight up in the air.

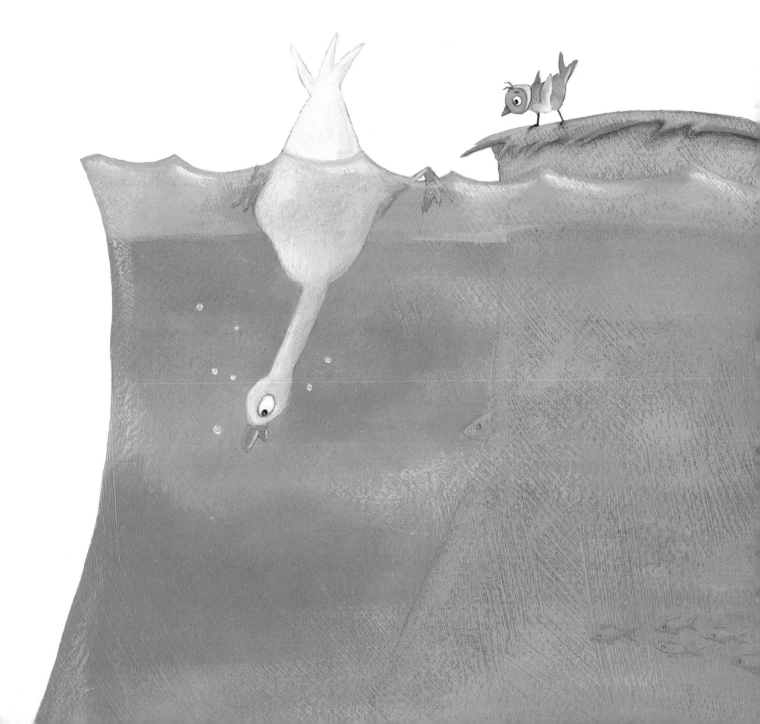

But she couldn't reach it either.
Dripping and drooping,
She came up empty-handed.

"That beautiful
red berry was for
her grandma," Sighed the chipmunk,
"and now She has nothing to give her."

Lori, the chipmunk, and the goose
Slouched on the riverbank
and thought for a while.

A flip-flopping frog flung himself
into their midst.

"Why so drab and droopy today?" he asked.
"Hip, hop, *plop!* Her beautiful red berry sank
right to the bottom of the river," explained
the goose, "and we can't reach it."

"No problem!" said the frog.

The frog
flipped
into the water,
flapped his
floppy feet,
flicked his fingers,
and swam to
the surface with the
strawberry
in his hand!

Hooray!

OH, NO!

Lori thought frantically.

Then she tossed her beautiful
red
berry
into the air.

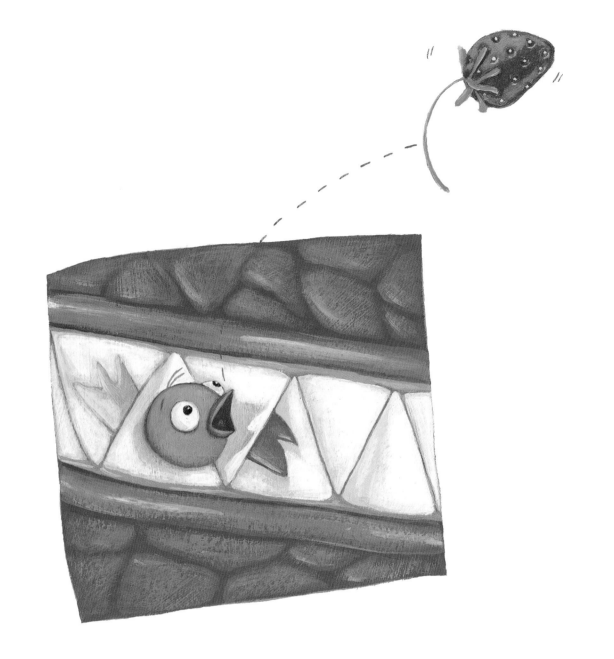

The greedy croc
   opened his mouth wide
to catch it,

and everyone escaped!

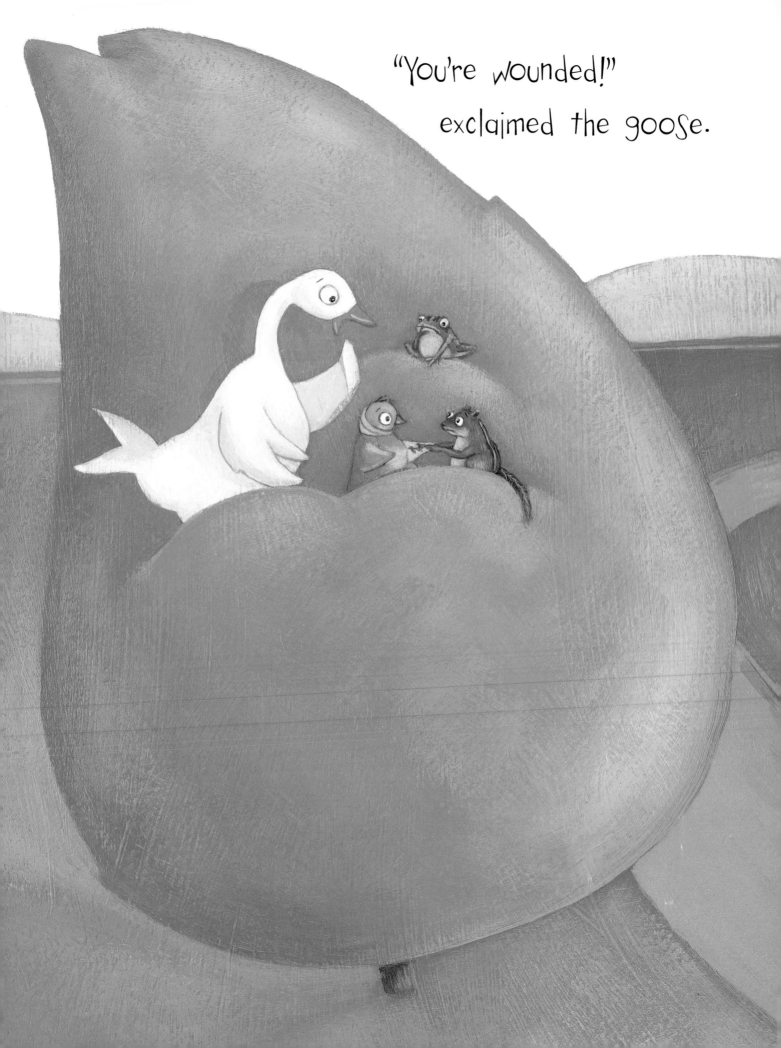

"You're wounded!" exclaimed the goose.

The chipmunk, the goose, and the frog tenderly nursed Lori.

"My beautiful red berry is gone for good," Lori sighed. "What will I give my grandma?"

Lori, the chipmunk, the goose, and the frog shivered in a tree and thought for a while.

Eventually,
Lori had an idea.

Lori, the chipmunk, the goose, and
the frog put their beaks and jaws,
feathers and paws together.

They got
right to work.

At last, the four friends stitched
together the story of their adventure.
Then they set off to visit Grandma.

"Hello! Hello!
Hello! Hello!"
Grandma sang.

"Ooooh! My poor little Lorikeet!
Whatever happened to your wing?"

Lori just smiled. She gave Grandma their gift.

"What a beautiful book!" said Grandma.

"Oh my!" Grandma gasped when she read the part about the crocodile.

But by the time she reached the
end of the story, Grandma was happy,
and so was everyone else.

"Read it again!" said Lori.